SLINGSHOT AND BURP

SLINGSHOT AND BURP

RICHARD HAYNES

illustrated by
Stephen Gilpin

CANDLEWICK PRESS

Text copyright © 2016 by Richard Haynes
Illustrations copyright © 2016 by Stephen Gilpin

First edition 2016

Library of Congress Catalog Card Number 2016937999
ISBN 978-0-7636-7076-4

16 17 18 19 20 21 BVG 10 9 8 7 6 5 4 3 2 1

Printed in Berryville, VA, U.S.A.

This book was typeset in Minion Pro.
The illustrations were created digitally.

Candlewick Press
99 Dover Street
Somerville, Massachusetts 02144

visit us at www.candlewick.com

To Megan
R. H.

For Tim, David, and Jeff . . . and our bikes
S. G.

CONTENTS

1
Rodeo Ride

Slingshot and Burp were Wild West cowboys—well, that's what they told themselves, anyway. They were looking for action. Heart-pounding action was their game. Danger didn't scare them, not one plugged nickel. If an F-5 tornado roared past, they would jump on and ride it like Pecos Bill.

Right then, Slingshot was eyeballing the scene from the back of his horse, Thunder (his bike, really, but who ever heard of a bike-riding cowboy?). "Boll weevil!" he said. "There's no action around here. Not even a dust devil to chase." Slingshot was born with ants in his pants and leaped after new ideas boots first.

"I learned to burp 'The Star-Spangled Banner,'" offered Burp. "Check it out. *Burp-burp-burp* can you *burrrrrrrp*—"

"Double aces! That's some good burping," said Slingshot, "but burping isn't getting us time in the saddle. C'mon. Time to find us a cowboy adventure."

"Hold your horses." Burp moved a tick slower than Slingshot. He liked to study a situation before charging in. "Don't you want to hear me burp the rest? What about 'home of the brave'?"

Slingshot and Burp lived next door to each other, which meant that their backyards bumped smack up against each other. The yards were mostly dirt and prairie-dog mounds and didn't have much more in them than a crooked swing set, two spiky cactus plants, and, toward a ditch at the back, a twisty cottonwood tree. Neither cowboy had ever poked a toe past that ditch. Out there was nothing but sand, rock, cacti, and coyotes. Straddling the two backyards was the only thing the cowboys really prized in that desert wasteland: the Rattlesnake Ranch Bunkhouse.

The bunkhouse was where the cowboys took a load off and gave their dusty boots a rest. Really, it was a playhouse that they were supposed to share with their big sisters, but snake spit, the girls hardly ever used it, so the boys took it over and stored their gear in it: bedrolls, bandannas, spare bike parts, canteens, you name it.

"We got everything?" asked Slingshot. "Cowboy boots?"

"Check!" said Burp, shoving a wad of beef jerky into his mouth.

"Cowboy hat and bandanna?"

"Check and check!" slurped Burp, giving his hat a tug.

"Horse?"

"Check," said Burp, throwing a leg over his own bike, Lightning.

"Protector?" Slingshot asked, raising his Super-X slingshot and taking aim at an empty can of baked beans. *Thwack!* That can danced across the dusty yard.

Burp pulled a Double-Barreled Spitball Blaster from his hip pocket. "Check," he said. He jammed chewed-up beef jerky into the ends of two oversize straws and took aim at the wounded can.

"Take that, you two-bit outlaw." *Thwap! Thwap!* That dented can spun in circles.

Something about the cowboys was even closer than their backyards. Their moms were sisters, which made the boys cousins. Believe it or not, the boys' dads were brothers, too. That made Slingshot and Burp double cousins.

Just then, the boys' older sisters, McKenzie and Kate, rounded the corner of the house. The cowboys liked to think of them as the Scorpions.

"Hey, cowburps," said Slingshot's sister, McKenzie. "FYI, Kate and I need the playhouse starting tomorrow, so get all your stuff out."

"It's not your playhouse. It's our bunkhouse," protested Slingshot.

"It's not YOUR anything," said McKenzie with pinched eyebrows. "It belongs to all of us, and you have to share. Like it or not, it's our turn."

"Yeah, we have important business to take care of," said Kate, Burp's sister. "So make like the Lone Ranger and ride off into the sunset." Kate blew a massive bubble-gum bubble and let it pop. "So there."

Howling with laughter, the girls turned and walked away.

"What do you think those two are up to?" asked Slingshot.

"Who knows?" said Burp. "I say, good riddance to bad varmints." He spit in the girls' direction.

"Yeah, good riddance," said Slingshot. "Ready to head out? I was thinking maybe it's time to mosey out into the Boneyard."

"The Boneyard! For real?" said Burp.

The desert beyond the ditch at the end of the cowboys' yards was called the Big Empty by most folks in those parts. Big Jim, owner of Boots and Saddle Tack Shop on Main Street, called it the

Boneyard. If Big Jim called it the Boneyard, Slingshot and Burp would, too. The way Big Jim told it, back in the Wild West days, many a cowboy had ridden out into the Boneyard, never to be seen again. Sure, a few turned up after a time, but only as a pile of bleached-out bones.

"What do you want with the Boneyard?" Burp asked.

"Let's go try and find a skeleton!" said Slingshot. "Just think, with a skeleton, we could spook the Scorpions all the way out of the bunkhouse and into tomorrow."

"I'd like to see that," Burp said, laughing. "But before we head out, let's make sure they know what's what." The cowboys hopped off their rides and got busy scribbling their brand on the playhouse with red crayon: RR in a circle. They also branded their bikes, boots, and belt buckles.

When there was nothing left to brand, the cowboys got back in their saddles and rode right up to the edge of the Boneyard. Although according to their dads it was little more than one square mile of dust, it suddenly seemed bigger than all of Texas.

"Maybe we better go talk to Big Jim first," said Burp. "You know, for some tips and stuff."

"Good idea," Slingshot agreed. "He'll know all the best places to find bones."

"Big Jim knows everything about everything," agreed Burp.

"Race ya there?" asked Slingshot.

"Race ya there," said Burp.

"Giddyap!" Slingshot charged off on Thunder.

Burp charged after him on Lightning, stirring up a swirl of dust. "Yippee!"

2
Big Jim's Lassos

Slingshot and Burp and Thunder and Lightning zigged around fire hydrants. They zagged around mailboxes. They charged down the bike lane on Main Street, past the Sinking Donut Coffee Shop and Slippery Larry's Reptile Farm.

They zoomed up to Boots and Saddle Tack Shop, hopped off their rides, and tore through the front door. *Mmm.* Their noses filled with a cowboy's favorite smells — leather, rope, and coffee.

"Whoa there, pardners," said Big Jim with a grin. "Where's the stampede?" Big Jim was a mountain of a man, with a broad, rugged face and a bushy, copper-colored beard.

"We're going to the Boneyard," said Slingshot.

"That so?"

"Tell us all about when you went there," said Burp. "We want to find a skeleton. But it's so big. And empty! We want to make sure we don't get lost and, you know, that we look in the right place."

The boys never knew for sure when Big Jim was sticking to the truth or stretching it, but one thing was certain: Big Jim was always good for an edge-of-your-seat story.

Big Jim handed each of the boys a mug of hot chocolate with a splash of real coffee in it.

"Mm-mmm!" said the boys after a sip. "Trail coffee."

"Let's see. Oh, I can tell you about the once

upon a time I was out hunting up rattlesnake eggs for breakfast and stumbled upon Windy Tucker's skeleton. That skeleton was stripped clean. Nothing left but bleached bones. Vultures and varmints had picked off every last speck of flesh."

"Whoa," said Slingshot, practically jumping out of his boots. "Who was Windy Tucker? Was he an outlaw?"

"Yep. And you know what else? When I found that old outlaw, he was still wearing his cowboy boots. His boots were hot-branded with the Flying W, Windy's brand. That's how I knew it was him."

Big Jim looked up at the shelf hanging high on the wall behind the cash register, the one he called the Shelf of Honor. On it sat a worn and cracked leather saddle, an old six-shooter, and a pair of dusty, cracked boots. Only one boot still had its spur, now rusted.

"You mean . . . that's them? Up there?" Slingshot pointed at the shelf. "Those are Windy's boots?"

"Yep! Those are Windy's boots and gear," said Big Jim.

"Weren't you scared when you found Windy's bones?" asked Burp. "Were you worried his ghost might find you and haunt you at night?"

"Burp," Slingshot interrupted, "are you cracked? A rattlesnake in his undies wouldn't scare Big Jim! Would it, Jim?"

Big Jim tugged at his shirt collar. "Well, now, a rattlesnake . . ."

"Where exactly did you find Windy's bones?" asked Slingshot. "Can you draw us a map?"

"Lookee here." Big Jim lifted a replica of an old "wanted" poster that he kept in a stack on the counter. He flipped it over and hand-sketched a map as he spoke. "From your backyards, go a short ways in past the stone shelves to that big one-humped Camel Rock. See? That's only about forty feet in.

"Go maybe a hundred feet more, past Dry Spring Gully, and you'll see a stand of old dead trees. From there, you're within spitting distance of the storm basin. That's Skull Valley. You should find plenty of bones there!"

The boys each took a swallow of trail coffee.

"Don't even think of going farther than that," Big Jim added.

Burp choked on a swallow of his coffee before asking, "W-why not?"

"'Cause then you'd be at the twisted canyons of the flattop mesas. That's . . . the Maze. That's one mixed-up place! It'll spin a compass cuckoo-crazy."

"Whoa," said Slingshot, leaning in.

Big Jim rubbed his beard. "'Course you might be interested to know, boys, that I only ever found half of Windy's skeleton."

"Half?" Burp repeated.

"Yep! The bottom half. The top half of him is still out in the Boneyard somewhere, crawling around, looking for his legs and his loot."

"Loot? You never told us about any loot," said Burp.

"Some secrets are best kept till the exact right time," said Big Jim.

"Is this the exact right time?" asked Slingshot, cracking his knuckles.

Big Jim took a long slow sip of coffee and leaned forward in his chair. "You bet your spurs it is!"

"Tell us everything!" said Slingshot.

"It goes back to a time when Windy was suddenly tossing money around town like it was horse feed. Some thought that maybe he'd hit the mother lode of all gold mines. There was only one problem with that theory: Windy didn't own a gold mine."

"Did he have a rich uncle?" asked Burp.

"That's exactly what Sheriff T-Bone Badger was going to ask him, but before he could, Windy lit out across the Boneyard on his white stallion, Avalanche. Next day, the sheriff got word that Windy was in fact the leader of the Tombstone Gang."

"Wow! Was the Tombstone Gang a bunch of outlaws? Did they rob banks and stuff?" asked Slingshot.

"They robbed anything that had money. Banks. Trains. Stagecoaches. Candy stores. Little old ladies' purses. You name it, they robbed it. And you know what, boys? Legend has it that Windy hid all that stolen loot in the Boneyard. It may be out there still."

Slingshot stared up at the Shelf of Honor. "Nobody's found the gang's loot yet?"

"Nope! And nobody ever found Sheriff Badger, either. He went off looking for Windy and never made it back. Some say the Ghost Cat ate him."

Burp gulped. "Ghost Cat?"

"Yep! Way I heard it, a nine-hundred-pound mountain lion snatched the sheriff right out of the saddle and ate him in three bites. Might have been the same cat what bit Windy in half."

"Is that true?" asked Burp. "Or just a rumor?"

"Half of all rumors are true. The other half could be," said Big Jim.

"Ghost Cat or not, Burp, we need to go look for that loot," said Slingshot.

"But a Ghost Cat . . ." said Burp.

Big Jim reached under the counter and pulled out two ropes. "Take these lassos. Just in case, you know, one of your horses should fall into a devil's slide —"

"A what?" Burp asked, bug-eyed.

"A devil's slide: a sinkhole. It can swallow a horse up right fast. With these lassos, you can rope your horse and pull him out without falling in after him."

"Wow! Real lassos," breathed Slingshot.

"Still living the cowboy code I taught you?" Big Jim asked.

The cowboys nodded, raised their right hands, and recited: "A cowboy is always ready. A cowboy helps anyone in need. A cowboy never gives up."

"Time for you cowboys to ride," said Big Jim. "Take full canteens. It's nothing but hot out there, and you can't drink hot."

"To the Boneyard!" Slingshot shouted.

"Loot, here we come," Burp hollered, trying hard not to think about the Ghost Cat, the devil's slide, or the other half of Windy crawling around in the desert, searching for his long-lost loot.

3
The Big Empty

The sun glared furnace-hot on the Boneyard. Sweat beaded across the cowboys' brows. Slingshot hitched up his pants and spit. The spit never made it to the ground; the scorching sun had sucked it dry in a bullwhip second.

"Did you see that?" asked Slingshot. "It must be over a hundred degrees out here."

"A hundred *and one,* at least," said Burp. "Hey, you think the Ghost Cat is watching us right now? Or maybe it only comes out after dark."

"Probably only after dark," said Slingshot.

The cowboys rode slowly to Camel Rock, looking in every direction. Three vultures circled overhead in search of a meal: something stinky, something dead.

"One way or the other, we're getting our bunkhouse back," said Slingshot. "Either we scare the Scorpions out, or we buy 'em out. So we need bones or loot."

"Yep!" Burp said, secretly hoping it would be loot.

The cowboys rode past leaning shelves of rock and tall cacti.

"What if the Ghost Cat is waiting to jump us?" asked Burp. "What if the Ghost Cat and Windy have teamed up? We could be vulture chow before sundown."

"Come on, Burp, stop being a desert turtle."

"What if we die of thirst? Or what if there's a wild horse stampede and we're trampled into dust? It could happen, you know," said Burp.

The cowboys arrived at a stand of dead trees and came to a stop. Skull Valley lay before them. Slingshot pointed to the wash past Dry Springs. "Map says that's where the loot and bones are."

"This place gives me the creeps," said Burp.

"Do you want to let the Scorpions steal Rattlesnake Ranch, Burp? Do ya?"

"No!" said Burp, inching closer to Slingshot.

Finally, after rounding another bumpy rock, the cowboys stepped into Skull Valley. Broken stones and hollowed-out, fallen cacti littered the desert floor. Crooked shadows stretched across the sand.

"It feels like a graveyard," said Burp. "And turn around — we can't even see our houses anymore."

"Knock it off, Burp. We're not even a mile from home."

From somewhere just ahead of them, a blood-curdling screech erupted, then echoed off the canyon walls.

"Ghost Cat!" yelped Burp. "Let's get out of here."

"We're safe in the daytime," said Slingshot, trying to sound sure of himself.

"Think there are any snakes out here?" asked Burp.

"They're everywhere," said Slingshot. "Under rocks, behind cacti, slithering sideways in the sand." He mopped his face with his bandanna. "Keep your eyes peeled."

The boys kicked over every small rock. They poked into every nook and cranny. Sweat almost burned the eyes right out of their heads. Burp jumped a bit every time a little lizard or bug scurried across their path.

"Boll weevil!" said Slingshot. "My mouth is as dry as a dust devil."

Burp pointed at a shimmering patch in the distance. "Look!" he said. "A lake!"

"That's a mirage!" said Slingshot. "Your eyes are playing tricks on you. Let's take swigs of water from our canteens and keep watching for snakes."

Burp took another gulp of water, and Slingshot loaded his slingshot with a pebble from the ground. If a sidewinder or diamondback jumped out — *thwack!* — he'd give it to them right between the eyes.

"Hold up," said Burp. "There's a saddlebag full of sand in my boot." Burp plopped down on a big rock and yanked off his boot. As he was emptying it, he

felt a tickle on his bare foot. He looked down and . . . froze. His lips were moving, but no words were coming out. Then, finally, "Giant . . . hairy . . . scorpion!" he squeaked, pointing at the dusty-brown critter perched on top of his left foot.

Slingshot acted fast. He snapped off a shot. The scorpion went flying! When it finally landed, that scorpion spun in a circle, then dashed off under a yucca plant to hide. Slingshot whooped and reloaded, but Burp was hopping up and down on one foot and clutching his shin. "It got me! It got me! I'm done for." Burp crumpled to the ground, still holding his shin.

"Let me see," said Slingshot. On Burp's left shin was a shiny red bump.

"I can feel the poison rushing through my blood," croaked Burp. "It's heading for my heart. I'm a goner." Burp jumped up, clapped his hands over his chest, and took off running for home. Minus one boot.

"Hey! Wait up!" Slingshot yelled. "Burrrrrp! Your boot!"

It was too late. Burp was tearing across the desert floor roadrunner-fast and showed no sign of stopping.

When Slingshot finally caught up to Burp, his double cousin was facedown on the ground in his backyard, still clutching his chest.

Looking up at Slingshot with hound-dog eyes, he whispered, "Take good care of Lightning for me when I'm gone."

"Burp, you're not going anywhere. That's no scorpion bite. The only thing that got you was the pebble from my slingshot. There's no broken skin. I swear! Take a look for yourself."

Burp examined the angry red bump on his leg. "You zinged me? Why'd you do that?"

"I was saving your life, remember? From the big hairy deadly scorpion."

"Oh," said Burp, sitting up. "Ouch!" He plucked a

cactus spine from his big toe. "Well, Big Jim sure was right about one thing."

"What's that?" asked Slingshot.

Burp yanked his boot out of Slingshot's hand. "That Boneyard is no place for tenderfoots."

4
Pink Eye

Back at Rattlesnake Ranch, Slingshot got an uneasy feeling. Something was not right. "Do you hear that?" he asked.

"Hear what?" asked Burp, ducking and looking around.

"That's just it. *Nothing*," said Slingshot. "Rattlesnake Ranch is too quiet."

"Oh, no. You're right," said Burp.

"Let's check it out," said Slingshot. "The last thing we need now is a girl ambush."

Slingshot and Burp crept over to the bunkhouse, staying low to the ground, then burst through the door.

Their mouths dropped open. "Jes-se James!" they wailed.

There were no Scorpion sisters to be found, but the entire inside of the Rattlesnake Ranch bunkhouse was swimming in pink, pink, PINK! Pink streamers hung from the ceiling. Pink curtains decked the windows. Even pink flowers peeked out from cracks between the boards.

A pink blanket in the middle of the table was piled with stuffed animals and dolls. Princess dolls. Rag dolls. Red-haired dolls. Frizzy-haired dolls. Brown-haired dolls. Dolls with bonnets. Troll dolls. Trouble dolls. Even dolls with lipstick, painted nails, and eyes that opened and closed. Lots of them had clips, ribbons, and bows in their hair. Half of them were wearing pink dresses.

"Buffalo barf!" said Burp.

"Rattlesnake Ranch is wrecked!" said Slingshot.

"Wouldn't you know it. We're out on a serious cowboy mission and they turn our bunkhouse into a crazy hair place. Come on, Slingshot. Let's show them who's boss." Each cowboy grabbed two dolls by the hair, hauled them outside, and lined them up on a bench.

The dolls sat there, all lined up and smiling and trying hard to look pretty. Slingshot studied them. "They look suspicious to me, like they know something but won't talk."

"Looks kind of like they're having a picnic," said Burp.

The cowboys looked at each other. "A firing-squad picnic!" they yelled.

Slingshot rushed into his house and came running back out with grapes. He loaded his Super-X with a plump purple one. Burp mashed up three with his teeth, then loaded them into his Double-Barreled Spitball Blaster.

"Ready. Aim. Fire!" called Slingshot.

Thwack!

Thwap! Thwap!

Ka-plunk!

"I love you!" said the frizzy-haired doll, tumbling over.

"Ready. Aim. Fire!" Burp called, and the cowboys fired again.

In the end, all four dolls lay in a twisted heap, covered in slimy grape goo. "Bet these pink outlaws were working for Ma McKenzie," said Slingshot.

"And her partner, Calamity Kate," said Burp.

"Aaaah!"

Spinning around, Slingshot and Burp saw two fist-clenching, teeth-grinding older sisters charging at them.

"Massacre!" screeched Ma McKenzie.

"Murder!" yelled Calamity Kate.

Before you could say cow patty, Slingshot and Burp were marched into court. It was the worst court any cowboy could ever be hauled into: Mom-and-Dad court.

Charge: Four counts of doll murder and destruction of doll property.

Verdict: Guilty.

Sentence: Grounded for two whole days.

"Two lousy days in lockup," grumbled Slingshot.

"Jail!" muttered Burp.

Two days felt like two years. When they were sprung, Slingshot had never been so happy to see his double cousin. He flopped down beside Burp on the ground. "Free," said Slingshot. "Finally."

Burp nodded and let fly a real belly belcher. "What'd you do in jail?" he asked.

"I went crazy and nuts both. I played checkers with myself, and I lost every single match. What about you?"

"I almost lost my marbles," said Burp. "I started thinking my pillow was making faces at me."

"I hate sitting in jail worse than sitting in a bubble bath," said Slingshot.

"Bubble baths are for babies," agreed Burp.

Slingshot and Burp spit at an ant that was crawling by carrying a dead fly. Their spit missed the ant but landed in front of four flip-flopped, painted-toenail girl feet.

"You'd better never touch our dolls again, Cow Pies," warned Ma McKenzie.

Slingshot shot rattlesnake eyes at the girls. "That's Slingshot and Burp to you, varmints. Take your dolls somewhere else. We want our bunkhouse back."

"Too bad. We're using it now," said McKenzie. "But don't worry. We piled all your old grubby stuff out by the tree." With that, the girls hurried inside the playhouse and closed the door.

A sign appeared in the window. It read: NO COWBURPS ALLOWED.

5
Squirting Skull

I'm so mad, I could bite a bone in half," said Burp. He burped an angry burp that wasn't even close to being any kind of song. "Ghost Cat or not, let's get to the Boneyard and find Windy's skeleton. We'll bring him back and scare the pink and giggle right out of those girls."

"Yeah! And when we find Windy's hidden loot, we can buy our own ranch," said Slingshot. "No girls allowed. *Ever!*"

Following Big Jim's map, the cowboys retraced their steps.

Slingshot mopped his brow with his bandanna. "We're in Dry Springs," he said.

Burp took off his hat and fanned his face. "Sure is longer without horses," he said.

"We must be close," said Slingshot. "Climb that rock and check."

Burp climbed up on a pockmarked hunk of sandstone and searched the horizon. "Hey, I see something glinting in the sun. It's them. Thunder and Lightning!"

In no time, the cowboys were back in the saddle, steering their horses around a sinkhole. They hadn't gone six yards when they came upon a bleached white skull leaning against a prickly pear cactus.

"Whoa! Check it out, Burp," said Slingshot, dismounting. "A real dead skull."

"I call first touch," said Burp.

"No way. I saw it first," said Slingshot.

"Doesn't matter who saw it first," said Burp. "First one to touch it owns it." Those were special double-cousin rules.

"Mine!" called Slingshot, diving for the skull.

"Mine!" called Burp, diving at the exact same time.

Slingshot elbowed and shoved. Burp yanked and tugged.

"Yow!" Both cowboys screamed when their knuckles smacked into the spines of the prickly pear cactus. Both boys let go of the skull and rolled around on the ground, coming eye to eye with the skull.

Essss! A low sandy hiss blew out of the skull.

"What was that?" said Slingshot, scrambling backward.

Essss!

"I'd say that was Windy's ghost!" said Burp, scrambling behind Slingshot.

"I dare you to get closer," said Slingshot.

"I *double* dare you to get closer," said Burp.

Slowly, carefully, they both leaned in and peered into the eye sockets.

Blood shot out — *splat!* — plastering each boy in the face.

"Aaah!" Slingshot cried, falling all over himself. "It burns!"

"It is! It is! It's Windy's ghost!" hollered Burp, tumbling over Slingshot in a rush to get far away from the haunted skull.

"Bluck!" he said, spitting. "It tastes like vulture vomit."

Slingshot shoved his face into Burp's. "You're covered in blood!"

"Hey! Don't kiss me," said Burp.

"Is my face smeared with blood, too?"

"Yeah! We both just got blasted by a ghost."

"Double aces! That's perfect!" whooped Slingshot.

"Perfect? Are you nuts?" said Burp.

"Don't you get it?" asked Slingshot. "We both got sprayed with blood. That makes us blood brothers."

"I thought you had to cut your finger or something," said Burp.

"Blood is blood. It's official."

"Wow!" said Burp. "That's even better than being double cousins."

The cowboy blood brothers shook on it, then turned back to the skull. The skull now sat silent as a stone.

"Cover me. I'm going in," said Slingshot. "If that skull moves so much as an inch, open fire."

"Got ya covered," said Burp, raising his blaster.

Slingshot moved a step closer. He took another step. And another.

Esss! The skull hissed. The hiss was followed by another bloody squirt. Slingshot dove aside, trying to avoid the spray.

"Maybe Windy is trying to tell us something. Maybe he really, really wants us out of here," said Burp, backing up as if to leave.

"But just think, Burp," said Slingshot, "how that squirting skull would freak the Scorpion Sisters right out of their skins."

Burp stopped in his tracks. "They'd run so fast, their hair would catch fire," he agreed.

"All we have to do is get the skull back to the ranch."

"Oh, yeah," said Burp. "Uh . . . how?"

"Just go ahead and grab it," said Slingshot.

"Me?" said Burp. "*You* grab it."

Essss!

"Aaah!" Burp about jumped out of his skin.

"I know. We can use the lassos," said Slingshot.

The cowboys wrapped the lasso rope around and around the blood-squirting skull, then wedged it between Slingshot's handlebars. Sister-scaring time was only minutes away. . . .

But when they roared back into the ranch, the girls were nowhere to be found.

"Why are they always here when we don't want them to be and never here when we do?" asked Burp.

"Because they're ornery varmints! Hey, I have an idea."

Slingshot first put on a pair of gloves, then set the roped-up skull on the ground and began unwrapping it.

Essssss!

"Watch it," Burp said. "Where there's a hiss, there's blood."

Slingshot stopped when the skull was still half-wrapped.

"Want to use it for target practice?" asked Burp, taking aim.

"Only if it shoots first," said Slingshot, crouching down for a closer look. "Hey, look! Something is moving inside the eyehole."

"Let me see!" Burp nudged Slingshot aside. "It's like a hairy eyeball. Maybe Windy's ghost is a blood-squirting zombie skull," he said nervously.

"Hey, watch it! It's popping out." Slingshot shoved Burp and they dove behind the wheelbarrow. *Plop!* A brown sandy lump sat next to the skull. It immediately puffed up to twice its size. *Essss!*

Burp covered his eyes with his arms. "W-W-Windy, stop scaring us. We come in peace. We're just regular cowboys, not the law."

"That's no ghost," said Slingshot, peeking. "It's some kind of prehistoric frog or something. Or a mutant gecko with spikes."

Burp uncovered his eyes. "Hey! I've seen one of them before. In a book."

"What is it?"

"It's called a horny frog. No, I mean horny toad. But horny toads aren't really toads—they're lizards. Those spikes are horns."

The horny toad's long tongue shot out and snapped up a passing red ant. *Gulp!*

"Wow! Did you see how fast it did that?" said Slingshot.

"Pick it up," said Burp.

"No way. You pick it up," said Slingshot.

Snap. Thwip. Gulp!

Snap. Thwip. Gulp!

Two more ants disappeared in a blink.

Slingshot took a deep breath, leaned over, and scooped up the horny toad.

"Whoa," said Burp. "You're braver than Wild Bill Hickok."

The horny toad lizard just sat there, in the middle of Slingshot's hand. There was no hiss. No squirting blood. It un-puffed, then blinked its eyes. Tiny drops of blood pooled in the corner of each eye.

"Hey! It must shoot the blood from out of its eyes," said Burp.

"Think we should keep it?" asked Slingshot.

"I guess, yeah! But it needs a name!"

"How about . . . Spike?" asked Slingshot.

"Nah! How about . . . Thumbtack?" asked Burp.

"Nah!"

They studied the pointy lizard in Slingshot's hand a little longer.

Burp burped a tune and finally said, "How about Bloody Eyes?"

"Double aces!" said Slingshot, slipping the lizard back into the skull's eye socket. "C'mon, Burp. We need to find the girls and let Bloody Eyes do some serious sister scaring."

"Shh!" said Burp, ducking behind the cottonwood tree. "I think I hear them coming."

6
Happy Tails to You

Sure enough, from around the side of the playhouse came Ma McKenzie and Calamity Kate, hauling the garden hose and some buckets.

"Look out, McKenzie," said Kate in a mocking voice. "I see the Burpsey Twins hiding behind the tree."

"Attack!" Burp shouted. He shoved Slingshot and the skull straight at the girls. "Attack!"

McKenzie dropped the buckets and turned the hose on them. The sudden blast of water knocked the boys sideways, and the skull fell to the ground.

"Is that old thing supposed to scare us?" said Kate, popping her gum.

"You'd better be scared," said Burp. "It's haunted!"

"We're not afraid of any old bleached-out bone," said McKenzie.

"Oh, yeah? Then I dare you to look closer," said Slingshot.

The girls nosed slowly in. McKenzie acted bored. Kate giggled nervously.

Esssss!

The girls froze. In the next blink, a squirt of blood came flying out of an eye socket.

"Aaah!" The girls screamed like fire engines, dropped the hose and the other bucket, and ran to the playhouse.

They yanked open the door. But before they could get inside, where it was safe, the playhouse erupted with barks, yaps, and howls. Slingshot and Burp were knocked over by a tornado of feet and fur.

"Stampede!" they yelled, falling to the ground and covering their heads with their arms.

Five frisky dogs jumped all over the cowboys.

"They're licking my face off!" said Burp. "Make them stop!"

"Princess! Sugarbaby! Trixie!" called McKenzie, laughing. "Come!" Princess and Sugarbaby, the two standard poodles, ran back to her side.

"First you pink our bunkhouse," said Slingshot. "Then you fill it with poofy clown dogs."

"It's our dog-sitting business," said McKenzie. "We get extra for grooming them. We practiced on our dolls, until you messed them up."

"We call it Happy Tails!" said Kate, kneeling and scratching Princess behind the ears. Purple bows were stuck to the top of the poodle's head. Two dogs had red nail polish painted on their claws. Another had ribbons and pom-poms dangling from its sparkly collar.

Only a small, frisky pup didn't obey the girls' commands. It kept darting at the boys and nipping at their ankles. It had bristly desert-brown hair, gangly legs, and pointy white-tipped ears.

"How come you don't have this one all junked
up?" asked Slingshot.

"That one," said Kate, clucking her tongue. "Can't
get him to sit still."

"He's got wild in him," said McKenzie. "Part
coyote."

"Here, boy," said Slingshot, tussling with the puppy. "You're not afraid of a little dirt, are you? I'll bet you just want to be free. You want to be a cowboy dog with us, don't you?"

"Guess what, Burp-Breaths," said McKenzie, scooping up the pup. "The dogs are staying with us."

"Yeah," said Kate. "We're staying with them in the playhouse. Overnight."

"And since you killed our dolls," said McKenzie, using a serious older-sister voice, "you two are on Pooper Scooper detail!"

"You're cracked!" said Slingshot. "We don't have time for any poop scooping. We've got plans of our own."

"We do?" said Burp.

"Yeah, we do!" Slingshot grabbed the skull and pulled Burp with him. "Forget them," he said. "They're crazy!"

"So what's our plan?" asked Burp.

The *plan* took a solid hour of begging, pleading, and promising. Their parents finally agreed to let the boys camp out in the backyard, but they had to cross their hearts and double-cousin solemnly swear not to bother their sisters in the playhouse. No matter what!

As the sun started sinking low, the boys spread their bedrolls beneath the cottonwood tree. It was cowboy camping at its best.

"You hungry?" said Slingshot. "Being on the trail makes me hungry."

"How about beans and beef jerky?" asked Burp.

"Every cowboy's favorite," said Slingshot.

"I'll grab it and be right back," said Burp, taking off for his house.

When Burp got back with beans and jerky, he pried off the lid and shoveled two cold heaping spoonfuls into his mouth. "Mm-mmm!"

"My turn," said Slingshot.

The cowboys snorted, howled, and burped out "Home on the Range," "Back in the Saddle Again," and "Don't Fence Me In."

"Double aces!" Slingshot hooted. "We're cowboys on the open range." They were so loud, they never heard the sisters coming.

"All your racket is stirring up the dogs," said McKenzie with a glare.

"And keeping us awake," said Kate, arms crossed and looking mad.

"You can't tell us what to do," Slingshot fired back.

"If the racket's not over in ten minutes, you'll be sorry," said McKenzie. "So pipe down!"

"Yeah, pipe down!" echoed Kate.

With that, the girls turned and headed back to the playhouse.

"Guess we'd better keep it down." Slingshot tilted his head in the direction of the playhouse. "We don't want to end up back in jail."

"They ruin everything," said Burp, popping a few knuckles.

The boys got quiet, nestled into their bedrolls, and closed their eyes.

"Hey, get your paws off me, Burp," said Slingshot.

"My paws?" said Burp. "How about you quit elbowing me!"

A wet nose and slurpy warm tongue startled the boys fully awake. It was the scruffy half-coyote pup.

"Hey, how'd you get out here, boy?" asked Slingshot.

"I bet he snuck out," said Burp. "You want to sleep out here under the stars with us, don't you, boy?" He gave the pup a piece of beef jerky, and the pup gobbled it up in one bite.

"A dog like this should be with us cowboys," said Slingshot.

"Yeah. He's a real trail dog. He's a cowboy's-best-friend kind of dog."

"First thing tomorrow, we'll take him with us to go after that loot," said Slingshot, fighting back a yawn.

"And to find the rest of Windy's skeleton!"

"Don't worry, boy," said Slingshot, pointing to the skull sitting by the old cottonwood tree. "We got Bloody Eyes to protect us while we sleep. Nobody will come near a haunted skull."

Burp burped out a soft chorus of "Burp, Burp on the Range." The boys' eyes grew heavy. The pup turned around in one full circle, looked up at the boys, and then settled down between them.

Under a sliver of summer moon, the three Wild West friends fell asleep dreaming of loot, bones, and running free.

7
The Boneyard at Night

At the edge of morning, an eerie screech jolted the boys awake. Through twisted branches overhead, they spied a white flash zooming by. It swooped low across the campsite, then soared up and out into the Boneyard.

"What was that?" asked Burp, sitting up.

"An owl, I think," said Slingshot. "Hey, where's the pup?"

Through the dark, a low whimper drifted in from the Boneyard. Then came a screech. A low grumble or growl followed soon after.

"Think that's the Ghost Cat?" asked Burp, shivering. "What if it already has the pup?"

"No! Don't say that. I'll bet the pup went after that owl," said Slingshot, jumping up. "Still, if we don't go get him — and fast — he might be nothing but a pile of bones by morning."

"But it's as black as tar out there," said Burp. A far-off yip and then a howl pierced the dark. Desert noises sounded bigger, more dangerous, in the nighttime. Both boys shivered, goose bumps running up and down their backs.

Pushing the fear down, Slingshot said, "That pup's in trouble! Cowboy code is: we have to help. Deal?"

Burp cracked his knuckles — *pop-pop-pop-pop.* "Deal," he finally said.

"And we can't ever, ever let the girls know the pup got lost," said Slingshot. "We can't even let them find out that he was with us."

"We'd be back in jail quicker than you can say

biscuits and gravy," said Burp, staring out into the endless dark.

Slingshot and Burp got out their flashlights. Slingshot and Burp *wanted* to go save the pup from the Boneyard. Slingshot and Burp *tried* to go to the Boneyard, but their boots had other plans. Their boots wouldn't move one inch.

"Maybe he'll come back on his own," said Burp.

"Yeah, maybe we just give him five more minutes," said Slingshot.

Another yelp sliced the darkness. "That's definitely him," said Slingshot. "Come on, we have to go save him. Cowboy code!"

This time their boots knew what to do. Without another word, Slingshot pushed into the pale darkness, Burp right behind him and nearly glued to his back.

Burp tried to switch on his flashlight. "Cow plop!"

he said. "It doesn't have any batteries! I bet you a million bucks Calamity Kate stole my batteries for her Goodnight Monkey clock radio. Again!"

"Shh!" Slingshot hissed, grabbing Burp's arm. "Hear that?" Another yelp came from just ahead. A spooky echo followed. "That was close."

Burp clamped a hand on Slingshot's arm and stopped. "What if the Ghost Cat ate the pup and now it's after us? What if it's licking its lips right now, hungry for cowboy steak?"

"Cut it out, Burp. You're making everything seem worse." Slingshot shook off Burp's hand and inched forward.

Burp stumbled after him, stepping on Slingshot's boot heels.

"Watch it!" gasped Slingshot.

"Here, boy! Here, boy!" they whispered, peeking nervously around every rock. Jagged shadows twitched and skittered in the low beam of Slingshot's lone flashlight. Every shadow seemed ready to pounce.

"This place gives me the creeps!" said Burp. "Windy's ghost is probably watching us right now. The Ghost Cat probably works for him, guarding the loot. I bet they lure cowboys out into the desert, just

to watch them squirm and turn into dried-up piles of bones."

"Knock it off, Burp," said Slingshot, shining the dull light in Burp's face. "My batteries are giving out. We have to hurry!" A new sound — a grunt — came from over by Camel Rock.

Burp reminded himself that home wasn't too far away, in case they had to make a mad dash for their lives. To be sure, he looked back and checked. The back-porch light of Slingshot's house still shone. So why didn't he feel one bit safer? Because if the Ghost Cat ambushed them, they would both be gone in two bites!

"If we don't find the pup in ten minutes, back we go. Deal?" said Burp, forcing his boots not to turn and take off for home.

"Deal!" said Slingshot. "Now, come on! Quit dragging your feet."

Arr! Arr!

The back of Slingshot's neck tingled. Razor-sharp claws of fear crawled up Burp's shaking spine.

"What if a pack of wild coyotes rushes us?" said Burp.

"Stop it! You're scaring the cowboy out of me," said Slingshot.

Suddenly they heard another noise. Or did they? In this kind of darkness, sound and distance — real and not real — got all mixed up.

Slingshot ducked behind a rock, pulling Burp with him. He whispered into Burp's ear, "Something's out here! Something big."

Just then, Slingshot's flashlight went dead. The batteries had finally given out.

8
Ghost Cat

Can *wild animals smell fear?* Slingshot couldn't remember. If they could, he thought he must smell like grilled buffalo burger!

"I'm g-going back," Burp stammered, pulling away.

Slingshot grabbed Burp's arm. "You can't leave!" Slingshot believed that sometimes cowboys had to make their feet go forward, even if they didn't want to.

Shaking in their boots, the boys nudged ahead, slow as snails.

Creeping through the dark, the cowboys were never quite sure if they were in real time, cowboy time, or Big Jim tall-tale time. Every dark outline of cactus became a ruthless outlaw. Every branch or twig became a diamondback ready to strike.

Burp never saw the dry gully right under his feet. Down, down, down he tumbled, on a roller coaster of stomach-churning fear.

"Yaaah! Quicksand!" he yelled. "It's swallowing me!"

Slingshot quaked. Quicksand was TROUBLE in capital letters. More than all the loot in the world, he wanted to be safe in his bedroll. And he wanted Burp snoring right beside him.

"*P-i-fff-i-t!*" Burp spit sand. "Help! Pull me out!"

Slingshot could just make out Burp's outline. "Grab hold of my hand," he called, leaning down into the gully.

On the count of *one, two, three,* Burp was up and out.

"That devil's slide almost ate me whole!"

Arr! Arr!

"That way!" The cowboys started off again in the direction of the yipping. "Here, boy. Here, boy." Why wouldn't the pup come?

Burp was so scared, he couldn't think straight. "What if that's not the pup? What if it's a trap?"

Slingshot ignored him and crept ahead.

Arr! Arr!

"I mean it," said Burp, digging his boot heels into the sand.

As he stood there for what felt like one long, endless moment, the sky was starting to show tiny hints of dawn. Burp had never been so happy to see the color pink in his whole entire cowboy life.

Feeling slightly braver in the pink light, Burp clutched his Spitball Blaster and followed Slingshot along a narrow, zigzagging path.

Arr! Arr! The tiny bark was always slightly ahead of them, just out of reach. What was the pup after? Or, what was after *him*?

Something like a branch snapped. Slingshot and Burp stopped cold.

The wind began to whistle. Dust whipped itself up into a funnel-shaped cloud and moved toward them. From out of the dust devil, a ball of fur came barreling at them. Burp screamed. The hair on the back of Slingshot's neck stood porcupine-stiff. This was more danger than even a famous cowboy like Wild Bill Hickok could handle. "We're done for," whimpered Burp, falling weakly to his knees.

"Ghost Cat!" Slingshot yelled, diving toward Burp and knocking him completely to the ground. The mini twister zoomed right over and past the cowboys. So did the ball of fur. Even in the panic, Burp recognized a flash of gray ears and tail.

"Hey, that was the pup!" yelled Burp.

Slingshot and Burp clambered to their feet and raced after the fur ball. It darted into a low rock overhang. The boys dropped everything and crawled straight in after it.

A new panic started to grow as they crawled into the cramped and tiny little cave. Still, they pushed and clawed farther as it narrowed, their hearts pounding jackhammer-fast.

"Come, boy! Come!" Burp pleaded. "Where'd he go? I can't see!"

Only a thin slice of gray light filtered into the crawl space. Slingshot groped and felt his way along the rough, jagged walls of the cave. "Hey, there's an opening here, all the way at the back. I can feel it, but I don't think I can fit through it."

"The pup must have gone that way," said Burp. "Here, boy. Come! Pleeeease."

There was no answer. Not even a whimper.

Slingshot slumped to the ground. A cold chill ran through him. He squeezed his eyes shut. In his mind's eye, he saw the Ghost Cat. With blazing eyes and sharp claws, it was coming. And it wasn't after the pup anymore. It was after them!

"We're done for," said Burp. "The Ghost Cat's going to crunch our bones like carrots."

Slingshot called up every bit of cowboy courage

he had left. "If that cat comes anywhere near the opening, blast him, Burp! Blast him into next week!"

Slingshot reached for his trusty Super-X. "Hey, my Super-X is gone! So's my flashlight!"

Burp went for his Double-Barreled Spitball Blaster. "Oh, no!" he said. "We must have dropped everything outside when we ran for it. We're sitting ducks now!"

4
Twisted Trail

A nerve-jangling, heart-stopping fear rattled the cowboys down to their RR-branded boots. The dark of the cave closed around them mummy-tight. From outside came another sharp cracking noise.

Was that the Ghost Cat, swiping its claws in after them?

"Help me dig, Burp. DIG! We have to find a way out."

If they didn't find an exit quick, that dusty hole might become a cowboy coffin.

The boys clawed and scraped at a small crack in the back wall until a big chunk of sandstone gave way and the cowboys tumbled into a bigger chamber with a clear opening straight ahead. Morning sunshine streamed in.

"We made it!" cried Slingshot. Just then, a different sound filled the air, a dry, rattling sound that seemed to ooze up out of the ground. The boys about swallowed their tongues.

"Rattlesnake den! Run!" Burp shouted, and took off, nearly flying right out of his boots. Slingshot was right there with him, scrambling for the opening.

Outside the cave, the boys flopped to the ground, gasping and thankful to have escaped Ghost Cat claws and rattlesnake fangs!

Turning his head to the side, Burp blurted out, "There he is!"

Just a few yards away, the pup sat near a tumbleweed, busily chewing on an old piece of leather. In the weak morning light, the scruffy pup looked full coyote. He looked happy, free, and wild!

"You scared the pork and beans out of us," Slingshot called to the pup. "No more call of the wild for you. Time to get you — and us — home. Pronto."

Burp pulled a piece of jerky from out of his pocket and held it out to the pup. "Here, boy!" The pup dropped the old piece of leather and trotted over to sniff at it.

"You're too young for the Boneyard," Burp said, scooping up the pup and cradling him under his arm. That hungry pup gave Burp's hand a big, wet lick. Then he started chewing on the jerky like it was candy. "Stick with us; we'll keep you safe."

"Wow! Burp, check it out," Slingshot shouted.

"What? Where?" said Burp, jumping.

"There!" said Slingshot. "Where the pup was!"

"I don't see anything," said Burp, scratching behind the pup's ears. "Quit scaring me."

Slingshot bent down and picked up something shiny. "It's an old buckle," he said. "And it's attached to a bit of leather." He let out a whistle. "I bet this is from an old saddle strap — a cinch or something."

"Let me see," said Burp.

Slingshot tossed the thing to Burp and began to scrape away at the sand some more.

A moment later, Slingshot whistled through his teeth again. "Whoa!" he said, holding up a twisted hunk of metal. "This is a . . . it's a spur. Windy's other spur! It's gotta be. And the cinch must be from Windy's saddle. We hit the jackpot! That pup's one lucky charm."

"Yeah," said Burp. "He led us right to it!"

"Wait until Big Jim sees this stuff," said Slingshot. "Let's go."

"But where are we? Nothing looks right. We came out the back end of that cave. I think we're lost."

"We can't be lost. We only came in a little ways."

But Burp was right; nothing looked familiar. Not the rocks, the cacti, or the lay of the land. No wonder so many cowboys never made it out of the Boneyard alive.

Slingshot looked east, west, north, and south. Finally, using the pink morning horizon as a compass, he said, "Come on. Follow me."

After five wrong turns, the cowboys came within sight of Camel Rock.

"There's the cottonwood tree!" Burp hollered, pointing with relief. "And home."

The cowboys tiptoed back to camp, trying hard to beat full sunrise and trying even harder not to be seen or heard by the Scorpion Sisters.

10
Jackpot!

"You're in trouble, mister." McKenzie stared daggers at Slingshot.

"You too, Burp-Breath," said Kate, arms crossed.

The boys were just crawling back into their bedrolls when Kate and McKenzie crashed into their camp, mad as wet cats. Burp quickly hid the pup behind his back.

"Where have you guys been?" growled McKenzie. "Instead of playing cops and robbers, or whatever it was you were off doing, you should have been here helping us."

"We should have been helping you with what?"
Slingshot asked. "We already told you — NO poop
scooping."

"Not that," said Kate, uncrossing her arms. "You
should have been helping us look for the runaway
pup. That half-wild mutt must have broken out last
night and taken off somewhere."

"We've looked everywhere," said McKenzie, "even in your bedrolls. Talk about gross." She held her nose. "Don't you two take your boots off before crawling into bed? Anyway, the point is, the pup has vanished. And it's probably your fault."

"Our fault! You're nuts," said Burp. "How do you figure that?"

"Because he probably followed you out to wherever you snuck off," said Kate. "Bet Mom and Dad would like to know where you —"

Right then, Burp started squirming and twisting sideways. The pup was licking every finger on both of his hands.

"Hey, why are you wiggling like that?" McKenzie asked.

"Yeah! What are you hiding?" said Kate.

Two dusty gray ears poked out from under Burp's arm.

"That's him!" shouted McKenzie. "Give him back, you dog nabbers."

Kate reached to take him from her brother. "How could you? Did you do this because of the playhouse?"

"Hang on, Burp!" said Slingshot. "Don't let them take the pup. They'll mess him up worse than a poodle or one of their frilly dolls."

"But that's our job," said McKenzie. "We get paid to give dogs makeovers. Then they aren't so dirty and stinky or, in his case, wild."

"But this one *wants* to be a cowboy dog and ride with us," said Slingshot. "He wants to be wild and free. Besides, we almost got eaten alive rescuing him, so we deserve to keep him."

"Give him back," said McKenzie. "His owners are paying us to wash the wild out of him, so stop playing cowboys. After his bath, we'll jazz him up and make him look like a show dog."

"That would ruin him. He doesn't want that. Why do you think he ran away?" said Slingshot. "Besides, you're the ones who lost him, not us. We saved him. Why do you think we even went out there in the dark?"

But the girls wouldn't listen. Kate reached out to take the pup from the boys. "C'mere, Jackpot," she cooed. "It's bath time for you."

The cowboys' eyes about popped out of their heads. *Did Kate just call the pup Jackpot?*

"What did you just call him?" asked Slingshot.

"Jackpot," said Kate.

"That's his name," said McKenzie.

"Jackpot!" said Burp. "That's just what we said when we found him out there in the Boneyard."

"Whoa!" said Slingshot. "I think the pup should stay with Burp and me. We're like three brothers from the same ranch."

McKenzie rolled her eyes. "Oh, brother. Now who's nuts?"

"I have an idea," said Burp. "How about we let Jackpot pick who he wants to be with?" Without waiting for the girls to say yes or no, he set the pup down on the ground between them.

The girls dropped to their knees. "Here, boy! Here, boy!" they called.

The boys dropped, too. "Stay, boy! Stay, boy!" they coaxed. Jackpot ran around in circles, nipping and fake-growling at the boys first, then the girls. Then he chased his own tail.

"Who's going to make you look pretty?" Kate cooed.

"Baked beans and jerky for breakfast—all you can eat!" Slingshot pleaded.

"Lemon verbena shampoo," McKenzie sang, "with lavender rinse."

"Red bows and green nail polish," Kate wheedled, flashing her nails.

"We'll give you bones," Burp promised.

The pup looked from the girls to the boys and back again. He sniffed the air and wagged his tail double time. Finally he bounced over to Burp . . . *Liiiick!*

"Hah!" said Slingshot. "He wants to be with us."

McKenzie shook her head and made a face. Then she and Kate huddled and whispered. Finally McKenzie announced, "You can borrow him . . . on one condition."

"Name it," said Slingshot.

"You have to promise to give him a bath and hand him back to us by noon tomorrow. That's when his owners are coming to pick him up. What do you say?"

"It's a deal," said Slingshot and Burp, crossing their hearts.

Grabbing the skull and Bloody Eyes, the boys ran off yippee-ki-yaying. Jackpot, that half-wild desert pup, chased after their boots like they were escaping armadillos.

"That was close!" gasped Slingshot.

"I thought for sure they were going to turn us in," said Burp. "We would have done two years in jail this time."

"Let's go show Big Jim the loot we found!" Slingshot said. "Windy's spur, Bloody Eyes, the skull."

"And don't forget Jackpot," said Burp. "He led us right to it."

"Just wait till Big Jim hears about our brush with the Ghost Cat," said Slingshot. "He won't believe that we almost had to take that cowboy killer on with nothing but our bare hands. C'mon! What are we waiting for?"

"Aw, I'm done for!" said Burp. "I can't move a muscle. Besides, Boots and Saddle isn't open this early."

Slingshot rubbed and polished the spur on his jeans, then held it up to the morning sun and whistled. "We were close, Burp. Close! And I've got a feeling the rest of Windy's loot is right near where we found Jackpot. It has to be." He pulled out Big Jim's map, studied it, and marked an X on the spot.

"And his bones," said Burp, yawning.

Just past the ditch, the cowboys holed up under a bush, hidden from any dead outlaws, howling mountain lions, or rattlesnakes. They set Bloody Eyes back inside the safety of the skull, then settled down with Jackpot for forty winks.

Hat over his eyes, Slingshot said, "After we catch some z's, it's straight to the Shelf of Honor at Big Jim's with Windy's spur. Then we hightail it back to the Boneyard for more loot."

"And bones," said Burp. "Don't forget the bones."

"Deal?" said Slingshot.

"Deal," said Burp. "Just as fast as Thunder and Lightning can get us there."